Published by Canon Press
P.O. Box 8729, Moscow, Idaho 83843
800.488.2034 | www.canonpress.com

Dr. Louis Markos, *Worldview Guide for the Aeneid*
Copyright © 2019 by Louis Markos.
For the Canon Classics edition of the epic (2019), go to www.canonpress.com/
books/canon-classics.

Cover design by James Engerbretson
Cover illustration by Forrest Dickison
Interior design by Valerie Anne Bost and James Engerbretson

Printed in the United States of America.

Library of Congress Cataloging-in-Publication Data
Markos, Louis, author.
Aeneid worldview guide / Louis Markos.
Moscow, Idaho : Canon Press, 2019. | Includes bibliographical
   references and index.
LCCN 2019011325 | ISBN 9781944503925 (pbk. : alk. paper)
LCSH: Virgil. Aeneis.
Classification: LCC PA6825 .M368 2019 | DDC 873/.01--dc23
LC record available at https://lccn.loc.gov/2019011325

A free end-of-book test and answer key are available for download at
www.canonpress.com/ClassicsQuizzes

17 18 19 20 21 22   9 8 7 6 5 4 3 2 1

WORLDVIEW GUIDE

The AENEID

Dr. Louis Markos

canonpress
Moscow, Idaho

For Robert Sloan
for helping to make Houston Baptist University
a place where Athens and Jerusalem
can truly meet

CONTENTS

INTRODUCTION

For 1500 years, Virgil's *Aeneid* reigned supreme. Whereas our self-conscious age has found greater solace in Homer's spontaneity than Virgil's sophistication, our ancestors found in the *Aeneid* a purpose, a pathos, and a profundity that moved them. It was Virgil—not in opposition to but alongside the Bible—who taught Christian Europe the shape of history, the cost of empire, the primacy of duty, the transience of fame, the inevitability of death, the pain of letting go, and the burden of adapting new strategies.

THE WORLD AROUND

The *Aeneid* is at once a timeless epic dealing with universal issues that cuts across all ages and cultures and a work of political propaganda that carefully and consciously reflects its historical moment. Virgil wrote his great paean to Rome in the 20s BC at the dawn of the Roman Empire upon the request of her first emperor, Caesar Augustus. Though Virgil does include subtle critiques of the emperor in the *Aeneid*, Augustus was for Virgil and most of the men of his generation a messianic figure who saved Rome from self-destruction.

Born in 70 BC, Virgil lived through a tumultuous period of civil wars that caused great social, political, and economic instability and led to the death of the Roman Republic (which had lasted 500 years). Like so many of his fellow Romans, Virgil looked on helplessly as two sets of strong competitive leaders (the First Triumvirate of Julius Caesar, Pompey, and Crassus; the Second Triumvirate of Marc Antony, Lepidus, and Octavian) fought each other for supremacy. These upheavals caused many once wealthy Romans to lose their patrimonies; Virgil himself came close to losing his.

When it seemed that Rome would tear herself to pieces, Octavian united the Senate against Marc Antony and his Egyptian consort, Cleopatra, defeating their combined naval force at Actium in 31 BC. For four years after that, Octavian maintained the illusion of the Republic, until, in 27 BC, he changed his name to Caesar Augustus (he was the adopted son of Julius Caesar) and ruled as emperor until his death in 14 AD.

Though he used brutal means to secure power, once he had it, Augustus brought stability and prosperity to Rome, instituting the *Pax Romana*, the "peace of Rome"— the longest reign of peace the western world has known. It was during this *Pax Romana* that Christ (the Prince of Peace) was born.

ABOUT THE AUTHOR

Publius Vergilius Maro was born in 70 BC; he lived a comfortable life and had good schooling. Unlike artists who must wait until after their death to be appreciated, Virgil was recognized all along as the great poet of his generation. He was patronized by Rome's first emperor, Caesar Augustus, who helped Virgil get back his land after it was confiscated during the civil wars.

Virgil was one of a coterie of writers whom Augustus and his wealthy friend Maecenas gathered to the court (today the name Maecenas is used to describe a patron of the arts). The group included the great lyric poet Horace, the epic historian Livy, and the comic-erotic poet Ovid. Augustus began his slow rise to power in the years following the assassination of his adopted father, Julius Caesar, in 44 BC. Again and again, he pressed the talented Virgil to write an epic about Rome in the manner of Homer's *Iliad* and *Odyssey*, but Virgil did not feel up to the challenge.

Partly to hold off the insistent Augustus, Virgil wrote two works of poetry: 1) a series of ten pastoral poems known as the *Eclogues* or *Bucolics*; 2) a four book mini-epic on farming and the Italian countryside known as the *Georgics*. But Augustus kept pushing.

Finally, starting shortly after the Battle of Actium (31 BC), Virgil devoted ten years to the *Aeneid*, often writing no more than 2-3 lines per day, finishing it shortly before his death in 19 BC (some argue, wrongly I think, that it was never completed).

The *Aeneid* was instantly canonized as a classic and was studied by schoolboys for almost the next two millennia. It is no exaggeration to say that Virgil's *Aeneid* is one of the most influential books in the history of western literature.

WHAT OTHER
NOTABLES SAID

Modern readers tend to privilege the raw, almost unconscious power of Homer's epics over the self-conscious artistry of Virgil's *Aeneid*. This shift began in the Romantic age with its privileging of novelty and originality; it is best evidenced in Percy Bysshe Shelley's rather startling pronouncement that Virgil, "with a modesty that ill became his genius . . . affected the fame of an imitator" and that his *Aeneid* must be refused the title "of epic in its highest sense."[1]

Still, throughout the classical, medieval, and renaissance periods, the *Aeneid* was considered *the* epic and Virgil *the* poet, as evidenced by Dante's decision to chose Virgil as his guide through Hell and Purgatory. Virgil may have lacked Homer's intensity, but he made up for it by his

---

1. Percy Bysshe Shelley, "A Defense of Poetry," in *Critical Theory Since Plato*, rev. edition, ed. by Hazard Adams (New York: HBJ, 1992), 525.

maturity: "No man who has once read [the *Aeneid*] with full perception remains an adolescent." This sentence was written by Medieval and Renaissance scholar C. S. Lewis, who follows it with a clear explanation of why Virgil's ascendancy lasted over 1500 years:

> Achilles had been little more than a passionate boy. You may, of course, prefer the poetry of spontaneous passion to the poetry of passion at war with vocation, and finally reconciled. Every man to his taste. But we must not blame the second for not being the first. With Virgil European poetry grows up. For there are certain moods in which all that had gone before seems, as it were, boys' poetry, depending both for its charm and for its limitations on a certain naivety, seen alike in its heady ecstasies and its heady despairs, which we certainly cannot, perhaps should not, recover.[2]

---

2. C. S. Lewis, "A Preface to *Paradise Lost*" (New York: Oxford UP, 1961), 37.

SETTING, CHARACTERS, AND PLOT SUMMARY

- *Setting: Various islands across the Mediterranean and North Africa, followed by Italy in the vicinity of Rome's future foundations, about 1200 BC.*
- *Aeneas:* Son of Anchises and Venus, chosen to lead the survivors of Troy to Italy
- *Anchises:* Father of Aeneas who escapes from Troy but dies in Sicily
- *Venus:* daughter of Jupiter and mother of Aeneas; she convinces Jupiter to help Aeneas to reach Rome, and her husband, Vulcan, to make armor for Aeneas
- *Juno:* Wife of Jupiter who resists Aeneas every step of the way
- *Creusa:* Wife of Aeneas who dies at Troy and prophesies Aeneas will marry again

- *Ascanius:* Son of Aeneas whom the gods name Iulus; ancestor of Julius Caesar
- *Dido:* Phoenician Queen of Carthage; commits suicide when Aeneas abandons her
- *Palinurus:* Friend of Aeneas; he dies as a sacrifice so Aeneas can visit underworld
- *Latinus:* Italian king who pledges his daughter, Lavinia, in marriage to Aeneas
- *Amata:* Wife of Latinus, enraged by a Fury when Latinus gives Lavinia to Aeneas
- *Evander:* Italian King of Greek origin who entrusts his son, Pallas, to Aeneas
- *Turnus:* Italian warrior betrothed to Lavinia; kills Pallas, then is killed by Aeneas
- *Sibyl:* Italian oracle and prophetess who leads Aeneas through the underworld
- *Nisus* and *Euryalus*: Trojan friends who mount a night raid; killed by Italians
- *Camilla:* Female Italian warrior who dies defending her land from Aeneas

The *Aeneid* begins with Aeneas and his crew landing on the northern coast of Africa, where the Phoenician Queen Dido has just established a colony at Carthage. Dido takes him in and, after dinner, he tells of the fall of Troy (Book II) and how he was rescued and commissioned by the gods to lead the surviving Trojans to Italy, where he will found a colony that will one day become the mighty Roman Empire. He also tells of his wanderings throughout the Mediterranean, in particular how he tried many times to stop and build his colony but was relentlessly driven forward by the gods (III).

Dido and Aeneas fall in love, and he plans to build his new nation at Carthage. But Jupiter sends Mercury to drive Aeneas away and finish his mission to found Rome. After Aeneas departs, Dido kills herself, swearing perpetual enmity between her descendants, the Carthaginian, and those of Aeneas, the Romans (IV).

Before landing on Italy, Aeneas returns to Sicily to hold funeral games in honor of his father, who had died there a year earlier (V); then descends into the underworld to meet his father's ghost and learn of the future that awaits him and his progeny (VI).

Book VII promises a swift ending to Aeneas's mission, as the Italian King Latinus, instructed by the gods, agrees to marry his daughter Lavinia to Aeneas and thus combine their two peoples. But Jupiter's wife, Juno, who hates the Trojans, riles up the anger of Lavinia's mother (Amata) and fiancée (Turnus). Civil war breaks out and Aeneas is forced to seek allies (VIII) among a Greek people group settled in a marshy land of seven hills, the future site of Rome. King Evander entrusts his son, Pallas, to Aeneas, and Aeneas's new forces arrive in the nick of time to help the Trojans.

Books IX–XII detail the extended civil war, focusing not only on the resistance of Turnus but of a female,

Amazon-like warrior named Camilla. During the war, Turnus kills Pallas, provoking the rage of Aeneas. The epic ends with Aeneas defeating Turnus in battle; he almost shows him mercy, but, when he sees the sword belt of the dead Pallas hanging from Turnus's armor, he kills him in a fit of rage. Before this, however, Juno and Jupiter agree that Trojans and Italians will merge their peoples to become Romans.

WORLDVIEW ANALYSIS

Although it is hypothetically possible Virgil could have read portions of the Septuagint (the Greek translation of the Old Testament), it is highly unlikely he did so. Yet, despite his ignorance of the Hebrew Scriptures, Virgil offers in his *Aeneid* an eschatological view of history that bears a striking resemblance to that presented in the Bible.

According to the Judeo-Christian worldview, history is not haphazard but moves forward in accordance with God's just but ultimately benevolent providence. Like an Aristotelian plot, history does not proceed randomly but has a beginning, a middle, and an end. Furthermore, in the Bible, that end is revealed to be a good one; indeed, the power of Christian eschatology (Greek for "study of the end") is that it takes an initially bad event and uses it as the basis for a good end. The Church Fathers referred to this eschatological transformation of evil into good as *felix culpa* (Latin for "happy fault").

Thus, the Fall of Man, surely a bad event, gives way to God's outpouring of love in the Incarnation: when God became man and entered our fallen world. Likewise, the Crucifixion, perhaps the darkest day in human history, led to the victory of Easter Sunday. The *felix culpa* aspect of this turn is evident in the name the Church has given to the day Jesus was crucified: Good Friday. For Christians, the Fall marks the beginning of history, the Resurrection the middle, and the hoped-for Second Coming of Christ the end.

According to Virgilian eschatology, history also has a beginning (the Fall of Troy), a middle (the founding of Rome by Romulus and Remus in 753 BC), and an end (the establishment of the Roman Empire by Caesar Augusts in 27 BC). Though the Fall of Troy was a terrible, bloody event that wiped out a city and a civilization, when it is viewed through eschatological eyes, it becomes a good event, for it leads, in the fullness of time, to the Roman Empire.

Virgil gives us a glimpse of this historical process when he comes to the Temple of Juno at Carthage in Book I. There he learns that Dido knew where to build her city because she was given a sign: the head of a warhorse. Attentive readers will take from this a symbolic key: whenever we see a horse in the epic, it represents the building of a city. So far so good, until we move on to Book II and discover that a horse (the fabled Trojan Horse) now symbolizes the fall of a city. At first it might seem that Virgil has lost thematic control of his epic, but he has not; from an eschatological point of view, the fall of a city and the rise of a city are intimately related, with one leading to the other.

The *Aeneid* shares a historical worldview with the Bible; as such, it also shares a similar understanding of what virtues a hero must possess if he is to succeed in a world so constructed. Given the slow, often imperceptible, development of the divine providential plan, the supreme virtue of the poem is faith. Virgil's heroes, like biblical believers, must put their faith in a grand design which they cannot see and which they will not live to witness the end of. As the Jews yearned and longed for the coming of the Messiah, and as Christians yearn and long for his Second Coming, so Aeneas yearns and longs for promises that will not be fulfilled for centuries.

Again and again throughout the epic, the travel-weary Aeneas wants to stop and build his city, but he is relentlessly pressed onward by the gods. While passing through Greece, he comes upon a miniature replica of Troy, led by Helenus, son of the late Trojan King Priam, and his wife, Andromache, the widow of the great Hector. Aeneas yearns to stay with them, but he knows that he must, like Abraham, continue on to the land promised him by the gods. "Be happy, friends," he says as he departs, "your fortune is achieved, / While one fate beckons us and then another. / Here is your quiet rest: no sea to plow / No quest for dim lands of Ausonia / Receding ever" (III.655–659).[3]

---

3. All quotes from Virgil are taken from *The Aeneid*, translated by Robert Fitzgerald (New York: Vintage Books, 1984). References will be given in the text by book and line number.

Still, despite the pain of moving on, Aeneas is sustained by the prophecies he has received and also by an Isaiah-and-Ezekiel-like vision that is granted him, even as Troy is being destroyed around him. Sensing Aeneas's reluctance to move on, his divine mother allows him to see what is really propelling history forward: "Look over there: I'll tear away the cloud / That curtains you, and films your mortal sight, / The fog around you" (II.795–797). In a flash of mystical insight, Aeneas sees that it is not the Greek soldiers but the gods themselves who are pulling down the walls of Troy. In the midst of what seems like chaos, there is a deeper purpose and a deeper plan.

Aeneas, we must remember, grew up in the world of Homer's *Iliad*. As Troy collapses around him, his first thought is to die fighting, exactly what Homer's Hector would have wanted to do. But that path is not offered to him. To the contrary, Aeneas is visited by the ghost of Hector, who instructs him to do the very thing that he (Hector) would never have done: "Ai! Give up and go, child of the goddess, / Save yourself, out of these flames" (II.387–388).

Like Saul of Tarsus, Aeneas is given the daunting task of becoming a different hero than he imagined he would be. Just as Saul the Pharisee would be transformed into Paul the missionary, so Aeneas the Trojan is forced to become Aeneas the proto-Roman who puts aside personal happiness and identity to serve a destiny he will not live to see.

When Jesus strikes Saul blind on the road to Damascus, he compares him to a stubborn donkey that kicks against the goads (Acts 26:14). Throughout the first half of the *Aeneid*, Aeneas plays the role of a recalcitrant jackass who simply will not bend his will to that of the gods. In the end, Aeneas surrenders and merges himself fully with his mission, but first he must lose his wife, father, lover, and friend (at the end, respectively, of Books II, III, IV, and V) and then, figuratively, lose his own life by descending into the underworld (VI). But then the transformation occurs: the defeated Trojan who goes in to the underworld comes out the appointed founder of Rome, ready to fulfill his mission.

Aeneas faces many trials and tribulations before he can emerge as the founder of Rome. The worst of those trials involves his leaving his beloved Dido. Modern readers have a hard time with Book IV, for we tend to privilege romantic love and personal happiness above all other things. The Romans of Virgil's day did not. For them, law, order, and unity trumped individual desire.

At the center of the *Aeneid* (and of both the Republic and the early empire of Caesar Augustus) lies the Roman virtue of *pietas*. Though this Latin word is the origin of our word piety, it does not connote an emotional or ecstatic love of the gods, as our modern word does. *Pietas* to a Roman meant the duty that one owes to the gods, to the ancestors, and to the Roman state. Love and marriage were not bad things in and of themselves, but their chief value was to bring stability and to instill honor.

Although the biblical worldview puts a higher premium on love than the Romans did, it nevertheless comes closer to Virgilian *pietas* than it does to modern individualism. The honoring of parents and of those in authority over us is as Christian as it is Roman, as is the vision of man, not as an autonomous individual with no ties or duties except to himself, but as a participant in something larger than himself: for Christians, the Body of Christ; for Romans, Rome as an idea, as the collective vision of the ancestors and of the Senate and Roman People (*SPQR*).[4]

Which is not to say that either Virgil or the Bible dismisses freedom and the dignity of the human person. Throughout the Old Testament and the *Aeneid*, the chosen people (the Jews; the proto-Romans) are set over against tyrannical powers that would crush and destroy their high calling to bring civilization and justice to the world. For the Jews, those powers include the Egyptians, Assyrians, Babylonians, Persians, Philistines and Phoenicians. For the proto-Romans, those powers are summed up in Dido, the passionate, barbaric foreign queen. She foreshadows both the later Punic Wars between Rome and Carthage—during the second of which (218-202 BC) the Carthaginian general Hannibal came very close to wiping out Rome—and the war against Marc Antony and Cleopatra that came close to destroying Rome again, but which was turned from defeat to victory by the

---

4. *Senatus Populusque Romanus:* the Senate and the Roman people..

messianic Octavian-Caesar Augustus at the Battle of Actium (31 BC).

Indeed, in Book I, Chapters 7 and 8 of *The Everlasting Man*, G. K. Chesterton makes a provocative link between the Jewish struggle against the Phoenicians (especially Jezebel and the priests of Baal who demanded infant sacrifices; see, for example, 1 Kings 18) and the Punic Wars between the Romans and Carthaginians (who were not Africans but an outpost of the Phoenician empire). God intended for the Jews to wipe out the evil and idolatrous Phoenicians, argues Chesterton, but they did not follow through. As a result, God used the pagan Romans to complete the job of wiping out Baal worship (Hannibal means "grace of Baal"). Once they did so, they established a form of justice and virtue throughout the known world, thus preparing the way for the coming of Christ.[5]

The quality of that justice and virtue was high indeed, and Virgil captures its essential nature in a passage that eerily reads like a quote from the gospels, though it was written almost a century before by a pagan poet who was ignorant of the God of the Bible. The passage comes in Book VI during Aeneas's meeting in the underworld with the shade of his father, Anchises. After reviewing with his son the future glory of Rome and extolling the virtues of the Roman heroes to come, Anchises admits to his son that in the arts of sculpture, rhetoric, and astronomy the

5. G. K. Chesterton, *The Everlasting Man* (New York: Image Books, 1955).

Romans will prove less skillful than the Greeks: "Others will cast more tenderly in bronze / Their breathing figures, I can well believe, / And bring more lifelike portraits out of marble; / Argue more eloquently, use the pointer / To trace the paths of heaven accurately, / and accurately foretell the rising stars" (VI.1145-1150). Just so did Virgil feel that he himself as a poet wrote constantly in the shadow of Homer.

But that is not where Anchises ends his speech. Yes, the Greeks had their arts and their giftings, but the Romans would bring another art and another gift to the world that would change it forever: "Roman, remember by your strength to rule / Earth's peoples—for your arts are to be these: / To pacify, to impose the rule of law, / To spare the conquered, battle down the proud" (VI.1151-1154).

The similarity of this to the *Magnificat* of Mary (Luke 1:46-55), in which she extols God as the one who "has brought down the mighty from their thrones and exalted those of humble estate" and who "has filled the hungry with good things, and the rich he has sent away empty" (vv. 52-53, ESV), is nothing short of remarkable. Rome, like the God of the Bible, will dispense both justice and mercy, now exalting the humble, now humbling the exalted. She will bring order out of chaos, and restore man to his original state. She will do this by being a steward rather than a dictator, by using her power for good.

Sadly, this high calling was fulfilled neither by the Roman Empire of Caesar Augustus nor by Aeneas himself.

On the final page of the *Aeneid*, as the defeated Turnus begs mercy from the triumphant Aeneas, the son of Anchises is given the chance to live up to his father's words. For a brief, shining moment, it seems that he will do just that; instead, he sees the belt Turnus had taken from the dead Pallas and is filled with wrath and revenge. He stabs the suppliant Turnus to death, thus foreshadowing both the civil wars that would destroy the Roman Republic and the founding of Rome by Romulus, who, according to legend, slew his own brother, Remus, to become sole leader (753 BC).

In *The City of God*, written in the aftermath of the sacking of Rome in 410 AD, Augustine famously contrasts the broken and sinful City of Man—founded on the fratricides of Cain and Abel and Romulus and Remus—with the holy City of God.[6] The former must eventually fall, and yet, as Virgil's *Aeneid* helped to convince the early and medieval Church, the God of the Bible (he whom Mary extols in her prayer) used the *pietas* of the pagan Romans, imperfect as it was, to prepare the way for Christ and for his true and eternal Kingdom.

---

6. Augustine, *The City of God against the Pagans*, ed. and trans. by R. W. Dyson (New York, Cambridge UP, 1998); see especially Book XV.

QUOTABLES

1. I sing of warfare and a man at war ...
                              so hard and huge
    A task it was to found the Roman people.
         ~ opening and closing lines of the prologue (I.1, 48–49).

"[Romulus] will take the leadership, build walls of
    Mars,
    And call by his own name his people Romans.
    For these I set no limits, world or time,
    But make the gift of empire without end."
         ~ Jupiter's prophecy of Rome's coming glory
    (I.372–375).

"Whatever it is, even when Greeks bring gifts
    I fear them, gifts and all."
         ~ Aeneas speaking of the Trojan Horse (II.69–70)

2. "Her holy things, her gods
    Of hearth and household Troy commends to you.

Accept them as companions of your days;

Go find for them the great walls that one day

You'll dedicate, when you have roamed the sea."

     ~ the ghost of Hector passes Trojan rule to Aeneas

(II.393–397)

"No pact must be between our peoples; No,

     But rise up from my bones, avenging spirit [Hannibal]!

     Harry with fire and sword the Dardan countrymen

     Now, or hereafter, at whatever time

     The strength will be afforded. Coast with coast

     In conflict, I implore, and sea with sea,

     And arms with arms: may they contend in war,

     Themselves and all the children of their children!"

     ~ Dido's curse on Aeneas and his descendants

(IV.868–875)

Vivid in the center were the bronze-beaked

     Ships and the fight at sea off Actium.

     Here you could see Leucata all alive

     With ships maneuvering, sea glowing gold,

     Augustus Caesar leading into battle

     Italians, with both senators and people,

     Household gods and great gods.

     ~ description of Battle of Actium on shield of Aeneas

(VIII.912–918)

21 SIGNIFICANT
QUESTIONS AND ANSWERS

1. How did early and medieval Christians view Virgil?

    Virgil was more than the greatest of poets to the
    early and medieval Christians. He was considered
    to be nothing less than a proto-Christian, one
    whom the God of the Bible used to prepare the
    Greco-Roman world for the coming of Christ.
    In fact, though the proper way to spell his name
    is "Vergil," Christians have long spelled his name
    "Virgil." Virgil with an "i" is a pun on Vergil and
    virga (Latin for [magician's] wand)—that is to say,
    Virgil is the Christianized Virgil, the one who was
    a sort of white magician. His *Aeneid* was held in
    such high esteem as a source of inspired wisdom
    that Christians up to the Renaissance would often
    open the *Aeneid* randomly and determine their for-
    tune by reading the first line of poetry that their eye
    fell on: a practice known as the *sortes Virgilianae.*

2. Was the *Aeneid* the major reason they considered Virgil a proto-Christian?

> Although Christians based Virgil's proto-Christian status partly on the *Aeneid*, an epic that embodies Christian eschatology and virtue, they based it even more on one of his earlier pastoral poems: the Fourth Eclogue. In this remarkable poem, written around 40 BC, Virgil prophesies the coming of a divine child who will bring peace and justice in words and imagery that make it sound like a passage from Isaiah. Though Virgil likely had Octavian in mind, early Christians were convinced that Virgil, without knowing it, had prophesied the coming of Christ. In fact, in many medieval Christmas plays, a character dressed as Virgil would read the Fourth Eclogue alongside passages read by David and Isaiah.

3. In what way is the *Aeneid* etiological?

> Etiology is the study of causes and origins, and thus the *Aeneid* is an etiological book; that is to say, it is very concerned with tracing the origins of Roman historical practices. Virgil's Romans, for example, worshiped household gods known as the Lares and Penates. Though the Trojans most likely did not worship such gods, Virgil includes a scene in Book II in which Hector entrusts household gods to Aeneas, commissioning him to carry them to the new city he will found. Virgil also finds numerous ingenious ways to trace Roman place names and family names back to characters and events in the *Aeneid*.

4. Can you give more examples of Virgilian etiology?

> In addition to the numerous small examples of
> etiology, Virgil includes in his epic the deeper
> causes of the two most defining events of the late
> Republic: the Punic Wars between Rome and
> Carthage (that lasted off and on from 264–146
> BC) and the Civil Wars (that lasted off and on
> from 133–31 BC). In the tragic love affair be-
> tween Aeneas and Dido (which could not have
> happened, since, even if they were real historical
> figures, Aeneas and Dido are separated by some 300
> years), Virgil located the true cause of the perpetual
> enmity between Rome and Carthage. As for the
> Civil Wars, Virgil traced that back to the struggles
> between the forces of Aeneas and Turnus, especially
> to Aeneas's vengeful slaying of Turnus.

5. Dido is obviously connected to Hannibal, but how is
   she also linked to Cleopatra?

> The Civil Wars of Rome ended with the showdown
> between Marc Antony (Julius Caesar's best gen-
> eral) and Octavian (Julius Caesar's adopted son).
> Antony would almost surely have won and become
> the first emperor had he not been brought down by
> his affair and alliance with Cleopatra, last pharaoh
> of Egypt. In Book IV, when Aeneas has his affair
> with Dido, he foreshadows Antony; when he heeds
> the gods and leaves her, however, he morphs into
> Octavian. Both Dido and Cleopatra represent
> for Virgil (and the Romans) the luxurious and
> corrupting influence of the East that would turn

noble Romans (like Antony) away from the path of virtue and *pietas*.

6. Is there a biblical parallel to Virgil's presenting Dido as the origin of the Punic wars?

> Were I to write a Virgilian-style epic about the ongoing strife between Jews and Arabs in the Holy Land, I would trace it back to the sibling rivalry between the two sons of Abraham: Isaac (the father of the Jews) and Ishmael (father of the Arabs and offspring of the Jewish Abraham and the Egyptian Hagar). Indeed, in a clever twist on etiology, Mohammed claims in the Koran that the beloved son whom Abraham almost sacrificed was not Isaac (Genesis 22) but Ishmael. Some examples of etiology within the Bible are the link between the Sabbath and God's resting from creation on the seventh day, and the twelve sons of Jacob becoming the twelve tribes of Israel.

7. How is biblical eschatology complemented by typology?

> In the Bible, God's eschatological plan for human history is given shape and focus through typology. For Christians, the Old Testament is filled with events and people that have full historical meaning in their own right but that also prefigure events and people in the New. Thus, the prophet Elijah, who wears sackcloth, lives in the desert on locusts and wild honey, and attacks the powerful but corrupt

leaders of his day (Ahab and Jezebel), prefigures (is a "type" of) the prophet John the Baptist, who also wears sackcloth, feeds on locusts, and attacks the powerful but corrupt leaders of *his* day (Herod Antipas and Herodias). The Exodus of the Jews out of Egyptian bondage and their eventual crossing of the River Jordan into the Promised Land under the leadership of Joshua is a type of the way Jesus (the Greek version of the name "Joshua") leads us out of bondage to sin and across the river of death into heaven (the New Jerusalem).

8. How does Virgil make use of typology?

For Virgil, most of the events and people in the *Aeneid* prefigure events and people in Roman history. In Book IV (see question 5), Dido is a type of Cleopatra while Aeneas goes from being a type of Marc Antony to a type of Octavian. Indeed, throughout the epic, Aeneas functions as a type of Caesar Augustus while his son, Iulus, is a type of Julius Caesar. That may seem odd, since the relationship of father–son is flipped when we move from Aeneas–Iulus to Julius Caesar–Augustus, but typology does not demand an exact repetition. The reason Virgil has the gods give the name of Iulus to Ascanius (the actual name of Aeneas's son) is to make clear the typological connection.

9.   How does Virgil take typology to a whole new, mythic
     level?

> When Virgil meets with his father in the under-
> world (Book VI), his father shows him a group
> of souls who will one day ascend to the earth and
> become the famous heroes of Roman history.
> Borrowing the concept of reincarnation (transmi-
> gration of souls) from Plato, Virgil suggests that we
> must return again and again to the earth until we
> gain fame (*fama* in Latin). The brilliance of Virgil's
> scheme is that it suggests that Iulus or Dido may
> not only be a type of Julius Caesar or Cleopatra;
> Caesar and Cleopatra may be actual reincarnations
> of Iulus and Dido.

10. What image embodies and explains the Roman virtue
     of *pietas*?

> The *Aeneid* includes a famous image that Romans
> of Virgil's day considered the epitome of *pietas*. In
> Book II, as Troy is burning to the ground, Aeneas
> goes to his home to rescue his father and his son.
> As Anchises is old and infirm, Aeneas lifts him up
> and carries him on his back. He then takes Iulus
> by the hand and the three make their way out. This
> image of Aeneas bearing the burden of both his
> ancestors and his descendants captures perfectly the
> meaning of *pietas*. Note that his wife is not part of
> the image. Though *pietas* does not exclude women,
> it tends to be a masculine virtue, placing duty about
> individual love and emotion. This is also true of the
> Roman quality of *virtus*, which is the origin of our

word virtue (often seen today as a more feminine quality), but which connotes "manliness" (*vir* in Latin means "man") rather than a passive kind of goodness and forbearance.

11. How is Aeneas a different kind of hero than Achilles and Odysseus?

Aeneas is, on the whole, a far less likable and charismatic hero than Achilles or Odysseus. The reason for this is not that Virgil lacked the literary skill to make him more dynamic and interesting, but that that was the kind of hero he was trying to create. The first glimpse Virgil gives us of Aeneas presents him as terrified, unsure, and longing for death. In the second glimpse, Aeneas calls on his equally terrified men to trust in fate and the future rather than in him (as Odysseus does in the same situation). Virgil risks a great deal in making Aeneas so flawed and indecisive, but he does so in order to make it clear that the real hero of his epic is not Aeneas but the eschatological forces of history.

12. Why should you prefer to be one of Aeneas' crew members rather than one of Odysseus'?

Although Odysseus is more charismatic, Aeneas is the more responsible captain. Whereas every single member of Odysseus's crew dies, Aeneas protects the men, women, and children who accompany him on his journey to Italy. Indeed, in a clever twist, Virgil has Aeneas, in Book III, save a Greek

sailor that Odysseus left behind on the island of
Polyphemus the Cyclops. What that means is that
the only member of Odysseus's crew who survives
is the one saved by Aeneas, he who embodies the
Roman virtue of *pietas*. There is, of course, another
reason for this disparity. For the *Odyssey* to have
a happy ending, only Odysseus needs to return to
Ithaca. In the *Aeneid*, if only Aeneas makes it to
Italy, he will have failed—for his job is to found
both a city and a nation of people.

13. In what way is the *Aeneid* a work of propaganda meant
    to celebrate Augustus?

The *Aeneid* is, at its core, a pro-Augustan work:
that is to say, it supports and celebrates the full
program initiated by Caesar Augustus. In keeping
with Augustan propaganda, Virgil presents the
newly established Roman Empire as the destined
end of 1200 years of history. Everything from the
Fall of Troy forward takes place for the sole and
single purpose of bringing Augustus and his *Pax
Romana* to power. Aeneas is chosen by the gods to
lay the foundations of that power, and he is assisted
throughout the *Aeneid* by every conceivable type of
god. In Aeneas, we see foreshadowed the *virtus* and
pietas of Augustus.

14. How does Virgil subtly include in his pro-Augustan epic criticisms of Augustus?

> Virgil makes it clear throughout the *Aeneid* that Aeneas is a type of Augustus. What that means is that every action that Aeneas reflects directly on Augustus. This typology becomes problematic in the second half of the epic when Aeneas proves unable to bring an end to the seemingly endless civil war with Turnus. As the body count mounts higher and higher, readers are forced to ask two troubling questions: is Aeneas (and therefore is Augustus) capable of keeping the peace and wielding justice? Is the Roman Empire really worth all the suffering it will take to achieve it? This anti-Augustan reading is brought to a head at the end of the epic when Aeneas kills Turnus in a fit of rage.

15. Can you give more examples of anti-Augustan passages in the *Aeneid*?

> In Book VI, Aeneas's journey into the underworld, Virgil includes at least three anti-Augustan elements: 1) Aeneas is told by the sibyl that if he is the chosen one, he will be able to draw with ease the Golden Bough from its tree, but, when he does so, the Bough resists him and he must tug at it; 2) when Anchises views with Aeneas the march of future Roman history, Virgil has that march end with the death of Marcellus, Augustus's virtuous nephew who he hoped (in vain) would succeed him as emperor; 3) when Aeneas leaves the underworld, he exits through the Gate of Ivory (which brings

false dreams) rather than through the Gate of Horn
(which brings true dreams).

16. How does the affair between Aeneas and Dido both
celebrate and criticize Augustus?

> As explained in question 5, when Aeneas leaves
> Dido, he ceases to be a type of Antony, who put
> his lust for Cleopatra ahead of his Roman *pietas*,
> and becomes a type of Augustus. Clearly, Virgil
> means us to be on the side of Aeneas in his decision
> to abandon Dido to found Rome . . . or does he?
> Rather than end Book IV after Aeneas's decision to
> leave, Virgil forces us to watch as Dido slowly and
> painfully loses her mind and commits suicide. Yes,
> we are on Aeneas's side—he *must* leave—but he
> does not need to "break up" with Dido in the cold
> and unemotional manner in which he does. Had
> Aeneas been more emotional and compassionate in
> his break with Dido (that is to say, had he been less
> "Roman"), perhaps he could have prevented making
> an eternal enemy of Dido and her descendants.

17. Isn't Virgil an inferior poet because he simply imitates
Homer?

> Though it is true that nearly every aspect of the
> *Aeneid* can be traced back to something that
> appears in the *Iliad* or *Odyssey*, Virgil's imitation
> of Homer is done both consciously and artistically.
> Virgil, far from simply "copying" Homer, reworks
> the earlier epics in such a way as to show the supe-

riority of Rome over Greece. Thus, although Virgil's divine pantheon is essentially the same as that of Homer, the gods of the *Aeneid* are far more serious and stoic than those of the *Iliad*. Unlike the gods of Homer, Virgil's gods never cry or laugh. It would be beneath their Virgilian (Roman) dignity. Yes, they are personal gods, as they are in Homer, but they are also forces of history who seem less intimately connected to the human sphere.

18. How does the shield of Aeneas differ from the shield of Achilles in *Iliad* XVIII?

On the shield of Achilles, Hephaestus engraves two cities that represent the choices we all must make. When Achilles goes into battle, he carries on his shoulder the full weight of our mortal choices and the consequences that go with them. On Aeneas's shield, in sharp contrast, Vulcan engraves the future history of Rome, with the decisive battle of Actium—which ended the Civil Wars and brought Octavian to power—depicted at its center. When Aeneas goes into battle, he carries on his shoulder not the choices we make, but the weight of history itself. If Achilles must bear up under choice, then Aeneas must bear up under *fate*.

19. How do the funeral games for Anchises differ from those for Patroclus?

> Whereas Achilles honors his friend Patroclus with funeral games (*Iliad* XXIII), Aeneas, in keeping with Roman *pietas*, uses the games to honor his father (*Aeneid* V). Furthermore, whereas Homer places his games near the end of his epic as a way to cool down the passions of war and the killing of Hector, Virgil moves his to the center, transforming them into a warm-up for the bloody battles of the second half of his epic. Finally, Virgil uses one of the competitions (archery) to comment on his relationship to Homer. The first archer shoots at the target (a bird attached to a string attached to a mast) and hits near the string; the second cuts the string; the third kills the bird. This leaves the fourth and final archer with no way of winning; still, in what seems a futile act, he pulls his bow and shoots his arrow into the sky. Miraculously the arrow catches fire, and he is declared the winner. Like the fourth archer, Virgil knew there was no way for him to "beat" Homer in the contest of epic writing, and yet, he made the seemingly futile attempt—and won: for over 1500 years, Virgil was considered superior to Homer.

20. Why does Virgil devote so much time to describing the Temple of Juno in Carthage?

> In Book I, Aeneas scans the walls of the Temple of Juno and discovers that they are engraved with the full story of the Trojan War. The surface reason

for this seems quite obvious: Aeneas is given the opportunity to survey his Trojan past before moving on to his Roman future. But there is a deeper, more subtle reason for this scene. Even as Aeneas scans the wall, Virgil the poet scans it as well. Like his hero, Virgil must review the poetic feats of the author of the *Iliad* before he can go on to write his own epic.

21. What double function does Palinurus play in the *Aeneid*?

In order to make his journey to the underworld, Aeneas is told that one person must be sacrificed. That person turns out to be the pilot of the ship, Aeneas's close friend Palinurus. Palinurus is a stand-in for Elpenor, a character who dies at the end of *Odyssey* X, seemingly as a sacrifice to clear Odysseus's way to visit the underworld in XI. Odysseus sees the shade of Elpenor in Hades and promises that he will give him a proper burial so he can find rest. In *Aeneid* VI, Palinurus makes the same request of Aeneas, that his body be given proper burial, but Palinurus is told that will not happen for a very long time. Still, the sibyl comforts Palinurus by telling him that a cape will be named in honor of him (modern-day Cape Palinuro). Aeneas overhears the sibyl's words, but does not yet realize that he too will only find his full reward when he is honored by his descendants as the founder of Rome. Such are the pains and the glories of living in an eschatological universe.

FURTHER DISCUSSION
AND REVIEW

Master what you have read by reviewing and integrating the different elements of this classic.

SETTING AND CHARACTERS

Be able to compare and contrast the personalities (including strengths, weaknesses, and mannerisms) of each character. How does the setting affect the characters?

PLOT

Be able to describe the beginning, middle, and end of the book along with specific details that move the plot forward and make it compelling. This includes the success or downfall (or both) of each character.

CONFLICT

Go through the character list and describe the tension between any and all main characters. Then, think about whether any characters have internal conflict (in their own minds). What is the purpose of the overt conflict (fighting), or any conflict with impersonal forces?

THEME STATEMENTS

Be able to describe what this classic is telling us about the world. Is the message true? What truth can we take from the plot, characters, conflict, and themes (even if the author didn't believe that truth)? Do any objects take on added meaning because of repetition or their place in the story (i.e., do any objects become symbols)? Be able to interact with and give examples for the following theme statements:

> Virgil's vision of the future (eschatology) is an Empire founded not on passion like Dido's Carthage, but on the virtues of courage, prudence, justice and self-control, exemplified by Aeneas.

> Virgil offers commentary on recent Roman histor-ical figures like Caesar, Cleopatra, and Antony by using his own legendary characters—Aeneas, Dido, and Ascanius—as types of future historical figures.

> The Roman idea of duty (*pietas*) was not the in-dividual's devotion to the gods, but meant duty to one's family, to the gods, and to the fatherland.

Finally, compose your own theme statement about some element, large or small, of this classic. Then, use the Bible and common sense to assess the truth of that theme statement. Identify your own key words or borrow from the following list as a starting point: *etiology; fame (is it worth it?); mortality; fate; individual passion; faith, hope, and patience; letting go of the past; revenge vs. justice.*

A NOTE FROM THE PUBLISHER:
TAKING THE CLASSICS QUIZ

Once you have finished the worldview guide, you can prepare for the end-of-book test. Each test will consist of a short-answer section on the book itself and the author, a short-answer section on plot and the narrative, and a long-answer essay section on worldview, conflict, and themes.

Each quiz, along with other helps, can be downloaded for free at www.canonpress.com/ClassicsQuizzes. If you have any questions about the quiz or its answers or the Worldview Guides in general, you can contact Canon Press at service@canonpress.com or 208.892.8074.

ABOUT THE AUTHOR

Louis Markos is a Professor of English and holds the Robert H. Ray Chair in Humanities at Houston Baptist University. He has written books such as *From Achilles to Christ*, *Lewis Agonistes*, *Apologetics for the 21st Century*, *On the Shoulders of Hobbits*, and many other books on classics, romantic poetry, and C.S. Lewis. He has written for *Christianity Today*, *Touchstone*, *Christian Research Journal*, *Christian Scholar's Review*, and many others. His modern adaptations of Euripides' *Iphigenia in Tauris*, Euripides' *Helen*, and Sophocles' *Electra* have been performed off-Broadway. He has also written a children's novel, *The Dreaming Stone*, in which his kids become part of Greek mythology. In the sequel, *In the Shadow of Troy*, they become part of the *Iliad* and *Odyssey*.